Dedication

This book is dedicated to Camden (aka Cam) who was born at 8:28 pm on February 2 – 8.59 pounds and 20.5 inches long. Cam is our third grandchild and second grandson. Cam - your smiles, hugs, and independent spirit are such special gifts to our whole family. Love you tons!!

Acknowledgements

My heartfelt thanks to:

- ◊ To my wife Pat (aka Nana) whose caring, nurturing, and unconditional love is such an amazing blessing to me and our family
- ◊ To Nicole whose grammatical touches provided easier reading and flow
- ◊ To Nancy who makes the publishing software look so easy; and
- ◊ To Mary who brought this story to life with her beautiful illustrations

D1711745

Introduction

This book is intended to be read to and/or with children. The instructions (or hope for this book) are simple:

- Invest a little *quality time* to nurture a stronger relationship with a child.

- *Model what matters*! Listening, imagining, laughing, and reading are ALL important.

- Do it yourself. Personalize the end of the book with your own stories.

So grab your bundle of curiosity, pure joy, and enormous energy. Sit back and go on a little 'adventure' with Camden and his family. I hope you enjoy!

Blessings,

Brian (aka Papa)

The sun was starting to set. Cam's eyes were getting very heavy. He had been riding in the car for a long time.

"It's okay to go to sleep", said Cam's Daddy, "when you wake up in the morning we will be in Florida."

"Papa and Nana already there?"

"Yes Cam," said Mommy, "and all your aunts, uncles, and cousins will be there too. It's our BIG family vacation!"

"Okay," and he quickly nodded off to sleep. Tomorrow he would be swimming and making sandcastles.

"Well, good morning sleepy head," said Daddy as he looked in the rear-view car mirror. "We are almost there. Cam, do you know where we are?"

Cam rubbed his eyes.

"Look out the window. What do you see?"

"The fish – the fish!" squealed Cam.

"That's right - just a few more minutes. Hope Nana and Papa saved us some breakfast."

"I hope it's chocolate chip pancakes," said Cam's older brother Evan.

"Me too," replied Cam.

"Cam, can you help me find the beach house?" asked Daddy. "Look for Papa's blue pickup truck. He drove it down this year to help us find him and Nana."

They went over several bridges, saw people fishing off piers, and spotted the big beach ball water tower. Then they turned on a side street toward the Gulf beach.

"There's Papa's blue truck!" shouted Cam.

"Great job, Cam!"

They were finally at their rented beach house. Daddy honked the horn twice and everyone came out to greet them and help carry things inside.

"Something smells delicious," said Cam's Mommy.

"Chocolate chip pancakes," replied Nana.

Cam and Evan looked at each other, smiled and licked their lips. "Yummmmm!"

After breakfast everyone headed to the beach. It was a very short walk. There, Cam played with his cousins (Reagan and Addison), made sand castles, and splashed in the waves. It was so much fun. Finally, Nana told everyone it was time to pick up and head back for lunch.

Papa said, "Cam please make sure you fill in the big holes where you were making sandcastles. The sea turtles don't like things blocking their path from the water to where they might lay their eggs."

"Sea turtles lay eggs?" Cam curiously asked.

"Yes, in a deep hole in the sand called a 'nest'. It's not like a bird nest made of twigs, leaves, and feathers. Female sea turtles can lay over 100 golf-ball sized eggs at one time – then cover them with sand to keep them warm. And, sea turtle egg shells are softer and rounder than a bird's egg."

"Wow!" said Daddy, "Where did you learn all that stuff – Papa?"

"Nana and I went to a sea turtle conservation center yesterday. We even got to see a sea turtle!"

Cam's eyes grew bigger. "A real live sea turtle?" he asked.

"Yes, and if you help us finish filling in these holes and catch up to everyone else I will tell you more about it. Okay Cam?"

"Deal, Papa!" Cam said with a big smile. Cam quickly smoothed out the sand.

At lunch Cam made a 'happy plate' and finished everything. Then he hopped back up on Papa's lap.

"Please tell me more about sea turtles, Papa."

"Okay, Cam. Here are some things I remember. All the world's turtles belong to one of three groups: sea turtles, freshwater turtles, or land turtles. Sea turtles:

- Are very, very old. They were around when dinosaurs were.

- Have flippers. Land turtles have feet with claws.

- Cannot pull their head or flippers inside their shell like land turtles do.

- Can hold their breath a very long time underwater (up to 5 hours).

"Can we go see a sea turtle – pleeease?" asked Cam.

"That's a great idea, Cam. Let's see if Evan and your cousins would like to join us."

"Ok." And, Cam went running off shouting, "Let's go on an adventure and see the sea turtles!"

All four older grandkids were excited and hopped into Papa's blue truck.

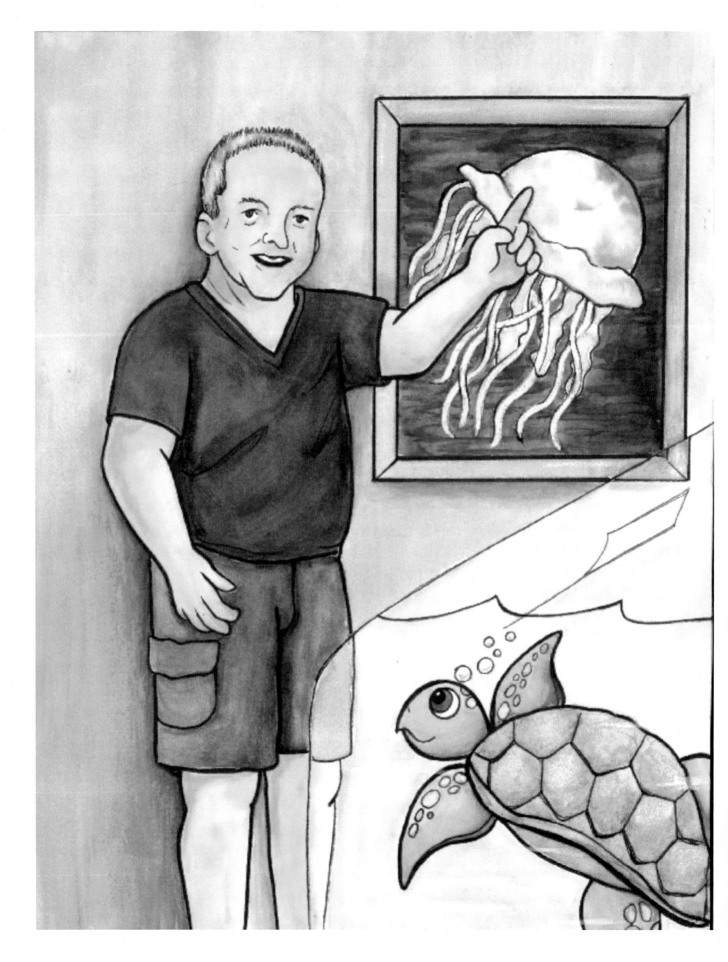

They drove to the sea turtle conservation center. There they met a volunteer named Al. He showed them how a mommy turtle uses her rear flippers to dig and cover her nest; what turtle flipper prints look like in the sand; what some sea turtles like to eat – jellyfish; and a real live Loggerhead sea turtle.

Volunteer Al also gave Papa a phone number to call for more information about where turtle eggs might be hatching. Papa called the number and talked to another volunteer named Michele. She told Papa a place near their beach house where they could meet her later that evening.

All the grandkids were super excited about the possibility of seeing baby turtles hatch – especially Cam. Every few minutes he would ask, "Can we please go see turtles now?"

That evening the whole family joined Cam's sea turtle adventure. Even Cam's two new baby cousins (Barrett and Nolan) went along. They drove about two miles and met Volunteer Michele near some bright flagging tape and stakes on the beach.

She shared what they should carefully do and not do around the nesting area. She told them that baby sea turtles, called hatchlings, usually:

- Take several days to dig their way out of their sand-covered 'nest'.

- Wait until night to leave their nest to avoid predators (like birds, crabs, and raccoons) that might hurt them.

- Leave in groups together.

- Use the reflection of the moon and stars to find their way to the water.

- Need our help or they may become extinct like the dinosaurs. For example - picking up plastic bags, so that sea turtles don't eat them and get sick, since plastic bags can look like jellyfish in the water.

Just then spots in the sand, inside the brightly taped triangular area, began to move like a pot of boiling water. Then a tiny turtle head popped out of the sand – then another and another and another. Soon there were so many tiny sea turtles that Cam couldn't count them all.

Cam's eyes lit up and he giggled with pure joy and happiness. His brother and cousins did too.

In less than 15 minutes it was over. All the hatchlings safely waddled and made it into the Gulf waters. Then they started their long swim to the seaweed beds to hide and grow. Everyone cheered and knew they had seen a 'God-wink' (little miracle) on the beach that night.

There were lots of baby turtle memories shared back at the beach house as everyone enjoyed their favorite bedtime snack – big, fat ice cream sandwiches.

On the last day of vacation, there was a knock at the beach house front door. A special delivery box had arrived. Everyone was very curious what was inside. Papa just winked and smiled.

"Cam, you get the honor of opening the box. You helped us create some GREAT family *life-long memories.*"

Cam quickly opened the box. The first thing he found was sea turtle t-shirts for all the kids. They quickly put them on. Next, he found puzzle pieces.

"Let's all put it together," Papa said to the grandkids and they joined him on the living room floor.

When they finished the puzzle, there were words in the center and lots of smaller pictures of their turtle adventure. Cam especially liked the picture of the baby turtles crawling into the water.

SOME LESSONS FOR LIFE

Sea Turtles:

- Can't hide their heads or tails in their shells.
  Remember - Don't hide from your fears,
  face them. Stand up. Keep your head high.

- Can hold their breath for several hours.
  Remember - Sometimes the best thing to do is
  not react right away but wait just a little longer
  (like sea turtles staying underwater) to be safe.

- Dig out of their nest at the same time.
  Remember - Many hands make BIG jobs
  easier and quicker.

- Come back to the same beach where they were born
  to lay their eggs.
  Remember - Wherever you go,
  you can always come home.

- Use the reflection of the moon and stars
  to find their way to the water.
  Remember - Even a little light in life
  can help you not trip and fall.

- Need our help and protection to survive.
  Remember - People do too!

The words on the puzzle were some lessons for life from sea turtles that Papa hoped Cam would always remember and most importantly practice. Some were easy for Cam to understand right now. Others would become much clearer as he grew up and older.

Finally, on the inside cover of the puzzle box, Cam found the last surprise. There was a special message from Nana and Papa. It said –

When pieces of your life puzzle just don't seem to fit - "*Trust in the Lord with all your heart and lean not on your own understanding.*" - Proverbs 3:5

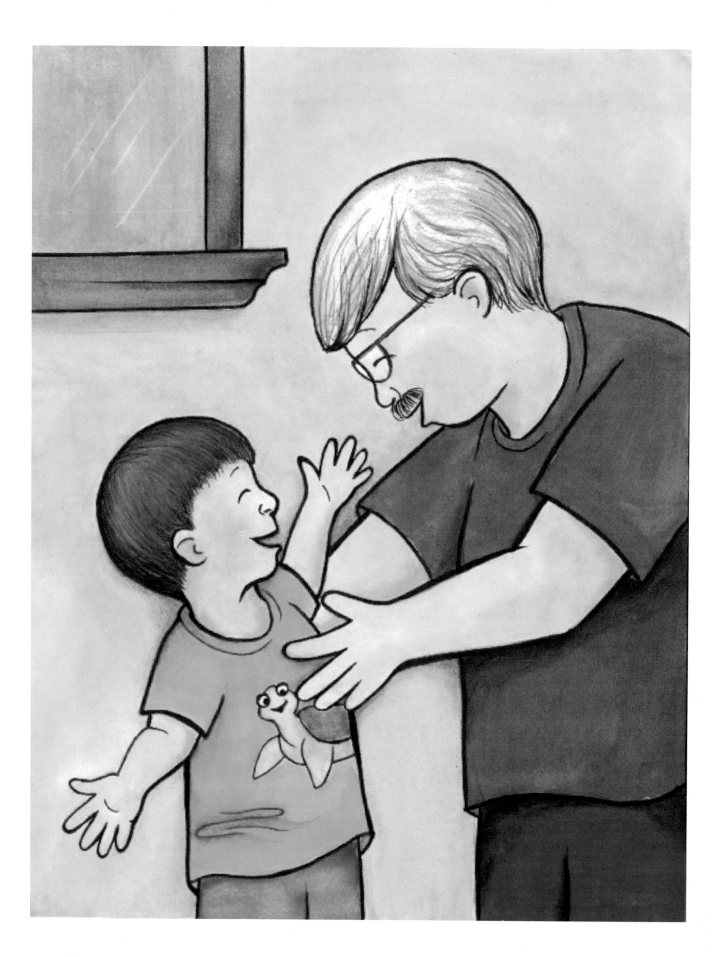

"Let's have more adventures, more fun!" Cam shouted.

"Let's make more life-long memories together!" Papa shouted back.

"More ice cream sandwiches too!" Cam's cousins chimed in.

Everyone laughed and agreed. They couldn't wait for their next family adventure.

What Do You Remember?

Please put your thinking caps on. Use the pictures on the opposite page to answer each question. CAN YOU FIND:

- Something very, very old that lived with sea turtles?

- A sea turtle's nest?

- A sea turtle's foot?

- What many baby sea turtles use to find their way to the water?

- Something that looks like a small plastic bag that some sea turtles like to eat?

- Where mommy sea turtles always go to lay their eggs?

Now It's Your Turn!

On the opposite page, document through words and pictures, those special adventures you have had with your children, nieces, nephews, cousins, or other special kids in your life.

Share some MEMORIES that can last a life time.

Special Adventures

Brian's Biography

Brian Gareau is a husband, father of three, and Papa to six (so far) grandkids. He is truly blessed with an amazing wife and family. He is a consultant, keynote speaker, and author.

For more information on Brian, check out his website at www.briangareauinc.com.

Crittenton Center's Crisis Nursery

We are proud to donate 10% of all earnings from Brian's children's books to this amazing non-profit organization that provides child abuse prevention services. For more information please check out www.crittentoncenters.org Other books in the series include: *Evan's Big Surprise* and *Reagan's Special Tree*. ALL can be purchased on Amazon.

How to Order this Book

Copies of *Camden's Vacation Adventure* can be ordered on Amazon.com. For large book orders (25+), keynotes and workshops, contact Michele Lucia at michele@briangareauinc.com.

Made in the USA
Columbia, SC
23 November 2022

71270176R00027